Maria Paints the Hills

by Pat Mora
illustrated with paintings
by Maria Hesch

Museum of New Mexico Press
Santa Fe

I run and run, and *swoosh,*
the wind lifts my kite.
It flutters and tugs at my arm.
I run home to tell Mother.

"Wake up. Wake up, Mamá! The needle will prick you." Slowly my mother opens her eyes, slowly like the heavy lids of chests. Sometimes she falls asleep over her sewing. She's tired.

"What are you sewing?" I ask.

"The canopy for San Ysidro." Mother says a canopy is a fancy covering we put over our *santo*, the patron saint of farmers. She says it's almost time for us to take San Ysidro out for a walk, to bless the fields.

"Why do we put a canopy over Saint Isidore?" I ask.

"To protect his head from too much sun, of course," Mother says. When we walk to the church, musicians play their violins and guitars and everyone prays that the corn and apple trees will grow.

My mother and I live in Santa Fe, New Mexico. Spring, summer, fall or winter, my mother sews.

"Why do you work so much, Mamá? Why can't you play with me?" I wish my mother didn't sew all the time, some days in the houses of rich families, and in our house too.

"Do your homework, Maria," Mother says, "or Sister Agnes will frown."

"You mean like this?" I say wrinkling my face like an old raisin.

"Maria!" says Mother. Mother is very polite. Not me. Sister Agnes says I like to talk and dance too much.

In the morning, I slip outside and look around for someone to play with. By the front door of our adobe house, I make some little people out of mud. When I can't find anyone to play with, I make or draw some friends. I sprinkle leaves, green and gold and brown, and then I hum so my mud friends can dance under the blue sky.

"Where are you, Maria?" calls Mother. "What are you doing? Are you talking to someone out there?"

"Come and look at the colors," I say. "Can't we go up the hills for a walk? Please, Mamá." My mother and I go collect flowers and herbs. "Look, Mamá," I say. "These flowers shine like diamonds."

When we return, Mother says, "Do your homework, Maria, while I warm some *posole* and beans." When I finish my school work, I start to draw with my old pencil. I wish we had a big house like my aunt and uncle's, where everything shines.

"Tonight we must go to bed early," says Mother. "Tomorrow is *día de los muertos.*" Every year on November 2, All Soul's Day, we go to the cemetery. We clean and decorate our relative's graves. Mother says it's a day for thinking about family. Mostly I think about my father. I never knew him, but I think he was handsome and had big, warm hands.

We get up early and fill buckets with flowers. We pack a lunch and collect rakes and watering cans. I scrub my father's grave and decorate it with the biggest and best flowers. At lunchtime, Mother and I put our blanket on the yellow grass. We munch *tortillas*. Mother talks with her friends about grandfathers and great-grandmothers. I hear families saying some prayers before they go home. We always say a special prayer for my father.

In the afternoon, the sun hides, and the sky looks gray and sad. I sit at the table while Mother sews, and I draw. I draw to make my mother smile. I draw the chile vendors bumping down our crooked streets in their covered wagons, and the blue jays gobbling piñon nuts. I draw mountains of onions and pumpkins and chiles and us making tamales with my aunts.

"*Umm,*" says Mother. "Your drawings make me hungry, Maria. I wish you had colors to draw the red and green smells of New Mexico. Maybe soon I can buy you some paints."

When the wind whistles through the bare branches, I like to go to my aunt's house, to the warm weaving room. Outside, the hills are white with snow, and the wind chases itself round and round. Inside, I play by the fire. Reina, the cat, stretches like a queen and yawns.

"Look, Reina," I say. "See the *caballitos* galloping in the fire?"

"What horses?" my aunt asks.

"Look, Tía," I say. "The flames look like little horses."

At night, snow drifts down again, quiet as feathers. Then, the wind arrives and shakes our house. When Mother and I are cold, she cooks us some *atole azul*. She stirs the blue cornmeal with water and adds a bit of syrup.

"That's all we have for dinner, Maria," says Mother, "but come and snuggle under the covers, and we'll drink our warm *atole. Ven mi niña y te contaré de otro niño.* Come, my child, and I will tell you about another Child." I snuggle closer to my mother.

Mother and I talk about how cold we were, walking for nine nights in the *posadas*.

"Tell me our pretend story about Christ being born in New Mexico," I say. "Tell me our story again, and I will draw it."

Mother says, "Suppose Christ was born in New Mexico instead of Bethlehem. Maybe Joseph and Mary were poor people from these hills, Maria. They stop to rest in an old shed of a nearby *rancho*. The shepherds, our shepherds, come down to see the new baby. They warm their hands over bonfires, *luminarias*, like we do on Christmas Eve. The wise men don't arrive here on camels, no. They arrive on horses."

I draw the ox and a *burrito* warming the Christ Child with their breath. Women bring pots of beans for the Holy Family.

On Christmas Eve after church, Mother and I shiver under the covers. I think of houses full of toys. I think of trains and dolls and little dishes. Then Mother hands me a present. I shake it and squeeze it. Mother laughs and says, "Open it, Maria. Open it."

I tear off the paper. "Paints! Paints!" I say.

Christmas Day I play outside in the snow, and when my hands get too red and cold, I paint at the table. I paint the hills and trees frosted with snow. I paint children with lots of presents in a big house that smells like Christmas, like cinnamon and chile.

Later, we visit my aunt's house. My cousin shows me her present, a new dress for the Easter dance, the *baile de cascarones.* At night I say, "When can I go to the *baile, Mamá?* Please. Let me go this year. Watch. Watch me. I already know how to dance. See?"

"Maybe next year," Mother says, "but in the spring, you can help your aunt make the *cascarones* for the dance."

When the days grow longer, we know spring is coming. Some days it snows, and some days the sun feels warm.

My *tía* says, "Maria, come and help us make *cascarones*." My aunt teaches me to pour the eggs out of their shells very carefully. After we wash the shells, I cut colored paper into small pieces and then put the confetti into the dried shells. We cover the opening of the *cascarones* with glue and paper. My aunt lets me decorate some of the eggs with my paints.

"Will men really smash these on the ladies' heads?" I ask.

My aunt laughs. "Yes," she says. "Oh, it's nice to have confetti decorating your hair, Maria. One day, you'll go to the *baile*, too."

The night of the *baile de cascarones,* I stand by the front door to hear the musicians tuning their violins down the street. I want to go watch the grown-ups dancing *La Varsoviana.* I want to see men buy *cascarones* and gently smash them on a pretty lady's head.

"Mamá, one day I want to have confetti all over my hair too," I say. "And I want to have a long, pretty dress and dance all night!"

"Come in now, Maria," Mother says. "Your aunt and uncle will take us out to see the spring lambs this week. You like that."

In the country, we all wave at the families plowing fields and making adobe, and my aunt tells me about the dance. My mother shows me the tiny lambs and says that soon our family will work together too. Every year, we help my Grandpa Charlie give his big house a good spring cleaning.

"Let's get to work," says Grandpa. "Who's going to whitewash the walls inside? Who's going to polish windows? Who's going to beat the rugs?" My mother and aunts scrub linens and stretch the lace curtains to dry. They wash the mattress filling and after it dries in the sun, Mother calls, "Maria! Maria! Come and help us to re-stuff these mattresses."

"Look, Mamá," I say. "See the clouds floating in the *acequia?*"

Soon school will be over, and I can play and paint all day. This year I can paint my kites. I'll watch the colors float up, up to the blue sky.

A note from painter Maria Hesch

 I was born in Santa Fe. Our home was on San Francisco Street, right across the El Santuario de Guadalupe. The Santa Fe River and Grandpa's alfalfa field were the only two things that separated us from the church. I lived with my widowed mother and next door to my Grandpa, Charles Conklin.

My mother, my grandpa "Charlie," his children, and my older sister were the dearest and greatest influences in my life. It was from them that I learned the stories, traditions, and customs that I have tried to portray in my paintings.

Our visits to my Great-aunt Delgado in her beautiful home on Palace Avenue also influenced me a lot. The visits to Uncle Henry McKenzie's ranch in Los Ranchitos de San Juan taught me all about rural life in New Mexico.

And so, with all these beautiful memories that I have from my childhood, I have tried in my humble way to pass them on.

Author's Note

Cynthia Farah

While living in Santa Fe in 1997, I regularly visited one of my favorite museums, the Museum of International Folk Art. How delighted I was when I saw a small exhibit there entitled, "A Kind and Gentle Life," featuring what the artist Maria Hesch had called her "primitives in the style of Grandma Moses." I was charmed by the images and immediately thought her work was perfect for a picture book.

Maria, a self-taught artist who was born in Santa Fe in 1909 and died there in 1994, was the daughter of Peregrina Delgado Campbell and James Conklin. Until her children "were grown up a bit," Maria did not devote significant time to her art. Then, in her words, she "got the nerve to start." She admired the work of another self-taught artist Grandma Moses because "her paintings tell stories." Maria's paintings do also. They tell the stories of the seasons and traditions of her rich northern New Mexico heritage, a heritage she helped to preserve.

My thanks to Bernice Hesch Chávez for her assistance with this book inspired by her mother's life and art. I am particularly grateful to Deborah Brodie for her early advice on this project, and especially to Mary Wachs, the witty and persistent editor who made the dream a reality.

To my friends Carolyn Trela and Gie van den Pol.
—P.M.

Project editor: Mary Wachs
Design and production: David Skolkin
Manufactured in China
10 9 8 7 6 5 4 3 2 1

Library of Congress Cataloging-in-Publication Data
Mora, Pat.
  Maria paints the hills / by Pat Mora; illustrated with
paintings by Maria Hesch.
    p. cm.
  ISBN 0-89013-401-4 (alk. paper)—ISBN 0-89013-410-3
(pbk. : alk. paper)
  1. Mexican Americans—Juvenile fiction. [1. Mexican
Americans—Fiction. 2. Mothers and daughters—Fiction
3. Family life—New Mexico—Fiction. 4. New Mexico—
Fiction.] I. Hesch, Maria, 1909–1994, ill. II. Title.
  PZ7.M78819 Mar 2002
[E]—dc21   2002069601

Museum of New Mexico Press
Post Office Box 2087
Santa Fe, New Mexico 87504
www.mnmpress.org